To Our darling Richy

We love you

Mum & Dad

Christmas 94.

The Moon Is Following Me

The Moon Is Following Me

by Philip Heckman

illustrated by Mary O'Keefe Young

Atheneum   1990   New York

Collier Macmillan Canada
Toronto
Maxwell Macmillan International Publishing Group
New York   Oxford   Singapore   Sydney

Atheneum
Macmillan Publishing Company
866 Third Avenue, New York, NY 10022

Collier Macmillan Canada, Inc.
1200 Eglinton Avenue East
Suite 200
Don Mills, Ontario M3C 3N1

First Edition
Printed in the United States of America
10 9 8 7 6 5 4 3 2 1

Library of Congress Cataloging-in-Publication Data
Heckman, Philip.
The moon is following me/by Philip Heckman;
illustrated by Mary O'Keefe Young. p. cm.
Summary: As they drive along in the dark, a child watches the full
moon follow the family car all the way home.
ISBN 0-689-31565-1
1. Moon—Fiction. I. Young, Mary O'Keefe, ill. II. Title.
PZ7.H3553Mo 1991 [E]—dc20
89-14921 CIP AC

To Cassie and Nicky, for this and other observations
P. H.

To Bridget and Andy, with love
M.O'K.Y.

It's after my bedtime when we leave. Gramma and
Grampa walk with us to the car, saying
      love you and
          drive carefully and
let us know when's a good weekend to come visit.

The light of the moon edges all of us in silver. Moonlight makes Gramma's smile gleam and Grampa's hair glow.

The moon backs up with us out the driveway. It has a big face tonight. It flies alongside the car, down familiar streets, following me home.

At first, city lights crowd the moon, but none is as white, none as round. Buildings try to block its way, but the moon slips behind them. I watch for it to jump out between the rooftops. Sometimes I'm ready and sometimes it surprises me.

Soon the city lights quit and fall behind. Only the moon can keep up with us. Nothing else can catch it; nothing can slow it down.

Now the moon rolls along telephone wires. It skips from
wire to wire without losing its balance. Underneath, its
reflection forms a net that moves across the grass, across
the river and the farmer's pond.

Tree branches tangle the sky. They reach and claw.
Silently, the sleek moon slips through their grasp.

We speed along the same path, except when the road curves. Then the moon takes a straight-ahead shortcut. When we meet again, it's as white and round and fast as before.

The moon nods at me as our car sways gently. I lean my
head against the window to watch the following moon. I see
my pale face reflected in the glass. The moon has washed
all color from the earth and hidden it away.

In the distance, dark wooded hills stand at attention. Tall black trees salute. But the moon rushes by without a backward glance.

The moon draws thin clouds like gauzy curtains across its face, making them glow like Grampa's hair.

Then it teases me, ducking behind and popping out of the growing clouds. Hiding, peeking, faster and faster. Until it disappears in darkness.

I open my eyes when the car stops. Pale moon faces loom over me in the bright light of night. My sleeping hand looks like a starfish in my lap. Stiffly, I get out of the car, blinking.

The moon followed me home while I slept. Somehow it
even got here before me. The same moon all the way.